Just So
Stories
for Little Children

Just So Stories
for Little Children

From the stories by Rudyard Kipling
Illustrated by John Joven
Retold by Anna Milbourne, Rosie Dickins
and Rob Lloyd Jones

Contents

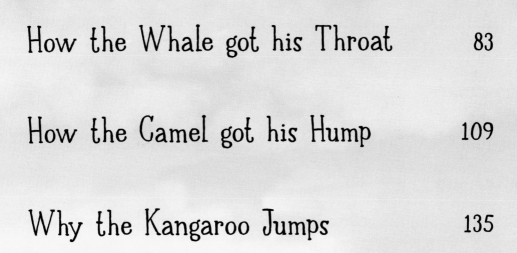

How the Elephant got his Trunk

Once, in a time long forgotten, dearest reader, elephants didn't have trunks...

...they just had short, stumpy noses.

This is the story of how those short, stumpy noses...

...became very, very long.

Baby Elephant was VERY curious.
He was always asking questions.

Why does Ostrich
have feathers?

Why does Giraffe
have spots?

One day, he asked, "What does Crocodile eat?"
"HUSH!" shushed his mother.

So Elephant went to see his friend Snake.
"What does Crocodile eat?" he asked.
"I don't know," Snake replied, "but you'll
find him in the great, green Limpopo River."

Then I'll ask him myself!

Elephant went down to the
great, green Limpopo River
and found Crocodile basking
in the shallows.

Hello Mr. Crocodile.
What do you eat?

Crocodile smiled a dangerous smile.
"Why, little Elephant, don't you know?"

"I...

eat...

ELEPHANTS!"

With a quick **SNIP SNAP**,
he caught Elephant's nose.

"**LED GO!**" squealed Elephant.
Crocodile gripped tighter.

Crocodile pulled as hard as he could.
"HELP!" cried Elephant. "I'm slipping."

A little white bird caught his tail.

Snake wound herself around Elephant's
tummy and held on tight.

Then Elephant, Snake and Little White Bird
pulled and **pulled** with all their might.

At last, Crocodile let go.
"Maybe I'll have fish today,"
he said and slunk back
into the river.

"Oh no," said Elephant. **"LOOK!"**

His nose had **s-t-r-e-t-c-h-e-d.**

It was a little sore
and very, very long!

24

"Don't worry," said Snake.
"A long nose might be **usssful**.
It's better than the mere **sssmear**
you had before."

Elephant's nose soon felt better. And, to his surprise, he **did** find it useful!

He could squirt water...

...brush pesky flies away...

...and pick
juicy fruit
from tall trees.

Told you sssso!

27

Elephant went home happily
and showed his family his new long nose.

Where did you
get that?

"Crocodile gave it to me," he told them.

When they saw how useful a long nose was, all the other elephants went down to the great, green Limpopo River...

...and they got long noses too!

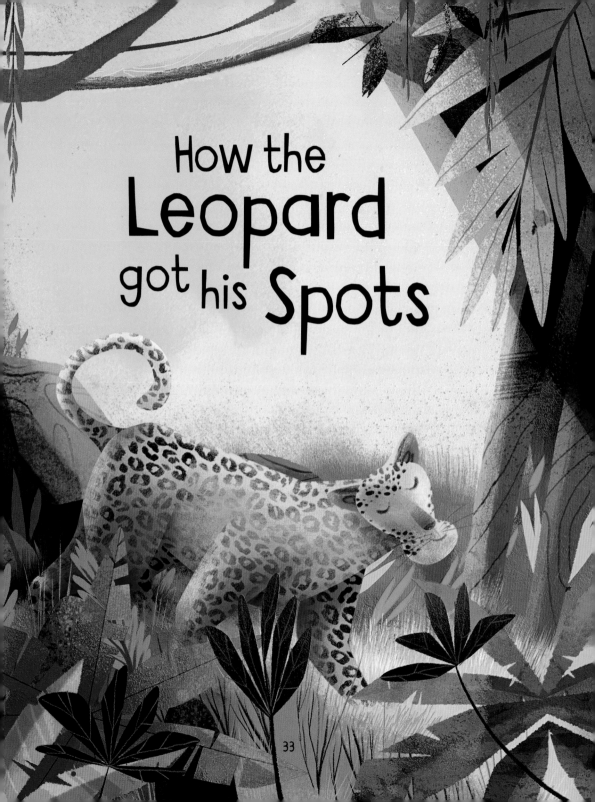

How the Leopard got his Spots

Long ago, when the world was new, the Leopard lived in a place called the High Plain.

It wasn't the Low Plain or the Medium Plain,
but the bare, hot, sunny High Plain.

It was full of sand and **sandy-brown**
rock and **sandy-yellow grass**.

Everyone who lived there was
sandy-yellow or **sandy-brown** too.

Leopard was the most
    sandy-yellowy-brown of all.
He matched the sandy-yellowy-brown
    plain to the last hair.

When he was hunting, he could sneak up
and surprise Giraffe and Zebra and the
other animals right out of their lives.

Searching for somewhere to hide, Giraffe
and Zebra came to a forest. It was a huge,
high forest, full of dark **blotches** and **patches**
and **stripes** of shadow.

Zebra and Giraffe spent so long among the
blotchy, patchy, stripy shadows, they grew
blotches and patches and stripes too.

Now they matched the forest
so beautifully, you could only
see them if you knew
where to look.

Out on the plain, Man and Leopard
hunted high and low together.

"I'm hungry," moaned the man.

Leopard's tummy grumbled
in agreement.

"I want meat!" he growled.

Grrrrr!

After ever so many days, Man and Leopard found the forest. They couldn't see much in the gloom. BUT THEN...

OOOF!

The man
walked into
something tall.

OWW!

Leopard bumped
into something
hairy.

"I've caught a thing
that FEELS like Giraffe,"
yelled the man.

"I've caught a thing that SMELLS like Zebra!" Leopard roared back.

Huh?

They dragged the things into
a clearing – and let go in confusion.
"You ARE Giraffe and Zebra! But WHY
are you so patchy and stripy and strange?"

"We'll show you," said Giraffe.
Zebra nodded eagerly. "WATCH!"

Giraffe and Zebra turned and
walked into the shadows.

One,
 two,
  three...

They **VANISHED!** Just like that.

Ha
ha
ha

Hee
hee hee

Muffled laughter drifted through the leaves.
"Where's your dinner now?" snorted Zebra.

The man rubbed his chin.
"That's a clever trick," he said.
I think I can do that too."

"HOW?" demanded Leopard.

"Like this," said the man. He took
a shadow and wrapped himself up
in it, so that he matched the shadows
around him.

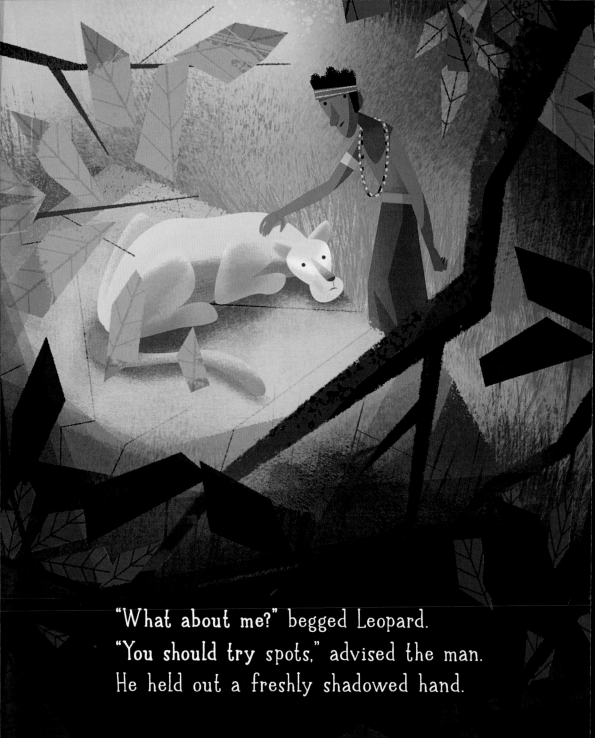

"What about me?" begged Leopard.
"You should try spots," advised the man.
He held out a freshly shadowed hand.

Dab, dab, dab!

He made shadowy fingerprints
all over Leopard's sandy-yellowy-brown fur...

...until it was **completely** covered in spots.

"Now you and I can hide in
the shadows too," said the man.

Since then, Leopards have always had spots.

And, if you look closely, the spots are always in
bunches of five — from five shadowy fingertips.

How the Rhinoceros got his Skin

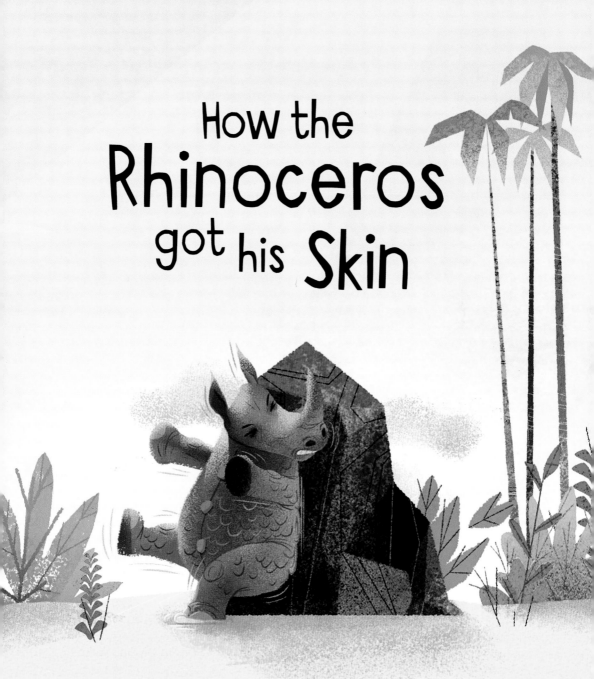

Once upon a time, rhinoceroses had horns on their noses, little piggy eyes and **tight, smooth skin.**

WHEEEE!

Their skin fastened underneath with
one... two... three buttons,
just like the buttons on a coat.

One rhinoceros in particular was
extremely **BIG** – and extremely **RUDE**.

He had no manners then
and he has no manners now.

HAH!

One day, this rude rhinoceros
smelled something sweet.
Something tasty.
Something that made
his mouth water...

It was a CAKE!

The rude rhinoceros ran at that cake and
he **spiked** that cake on the horn of his nose.

Then he galloped away and gobbled it up.

The cake-maker muttered
and tutted and collected
the crumbs.

"Them that takes cakes,
  which someone else bakes,
    makes dreadful mistakes," he warned.

The man watched
and he waited.

A few weeks later, there was
a heatwave. The sun beat down.
It got hotter and **hotter** and **hotter**.

The sea looked cool and blue and inviting.
"Time for a swim," thought the rhinoceros.

He unbuttoned his skin and left it
in a heap. Then he waddled out,
to **splish-splosh-splash**
among the waves.

Splish!

Splosh!

Splash!

The rhinoceros blew bubbles
and made water spouts.

He didn't notice the man
    take that skin and shake that skin,
        rub that skin and scrub that skin,

        and fill it full of old, dry,
        TICKLY cake crumbs.

Refreshed, the rhinoceros
climbed back into his skin.

Only now the skin itched and tickled
from all those CRUMBS.

GAH!

When he tried to scratch, it itched
and tickled even MORE.

He **rolled** and
rolled, down
sandy dunes.

He **rubbed** and **rubbed**,
against jagged rocks.

GRUNT!

But it didn't stop that tickle, **not one little bit**.

GRRR!

Then his skin snagged on a branch,
so he tugged. He **tugged** and **tugged**,
until his skin **stretched** and
his buttons **strained**...

PING!

PING!

PING!

DISASTER! He tugged SO hard that
his buttons popped off.

The rhinoceros gazed down
at his tummy in horror.

"**OH NO!**" he wailed.
"Now I'll **never** be able to take off my skin."

AARGH!

And **still** those cake crumbs itched
and **scratched** and **tickled** him.

From that day to this, the rhinoceros has had saggy, baggy skin, and a **VERY BAD TEMPER** – on account of all those crusty old crumbs.

But he **never** stole another cake again.

How the Whale got his Throat

Once upon a time, Whale was the GREEDIEST creature alive.

He swam around in the sea, eating absolutely **anything and everything** he saw.

He gobbled up snippy-snappy crabs...

...and gulped down spiky starfish.

He slurped long,
slippery silver fish...

and swallowed thousands
of glimmery golden fish.

One clever little fish hid behind
his ear, so she couldn't be eaten.

"HEY, GREEDY GUTS!"

she called out to Whale.

"If you don't slow down, you'll gobble up
EVERY LAST THING that lives in the sea,"
the clever little fish said crossly.

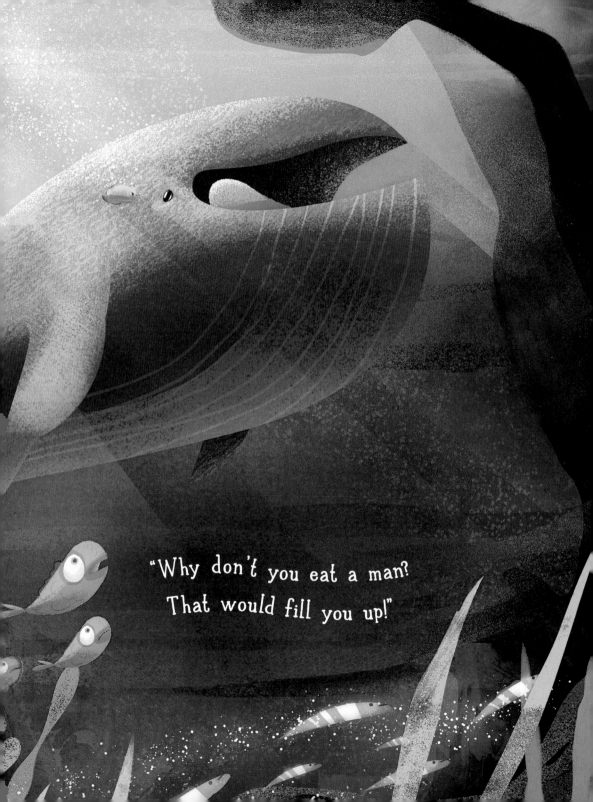

"Why don't you eat a man?
That would fill you up!"

"Yum, that sounds good," boomed Whale. "But where can I get one?"

"I'll take you to one," said the clever little fish. "So long as you promise not to eat ME."

They swam together across the
sea, until they came to a man
on a raft.

"There's one,"
said the clever little fish.
"Eat him, if you **dare**!"

"YOU BET!" said Whale eagerly.

He opened his
colossal,
gigantic,
ENORMOUS
mouth and...

...swallowed the man
and his raft whole,
in one great GULP!

Well, the man didn't stand for being eaten.
He **danced** and he **jumped**...

...and he **banged** and he **bumped**...

...and he thrashed and he thumped
inside the belly of Whale.

Whale groaned.

"It hurts! Oh why did I swallow a whole man?"

he moaned to the clever little fish.

"Come out, Man, come out!"

"Take me to land first,"
called the man from inside Whale's belly.

Thrashing his great tail,
Whale swam and swam all the way
across the wide, blue ocean...

...until at last he came to land.

The clever little fish came too.
(She wanted to see what would happen next!)

Meanwhile, inside Whale's belly, the man was busy.

He cut up his raft...

...made a big criss-cross shape,
and tied it all together.

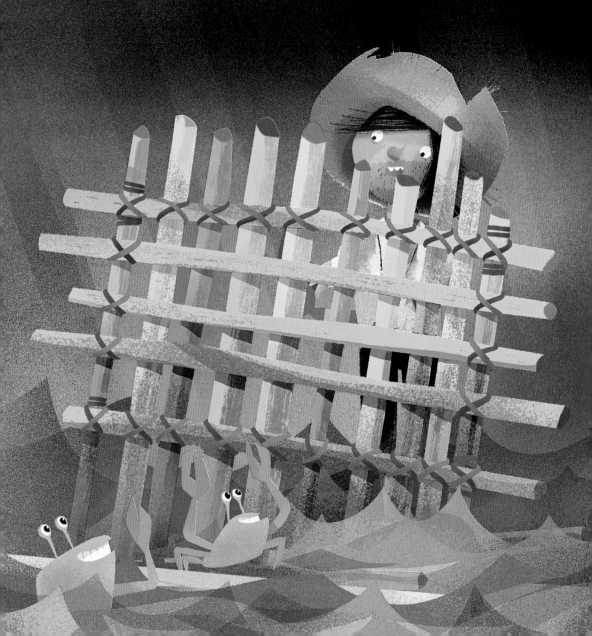

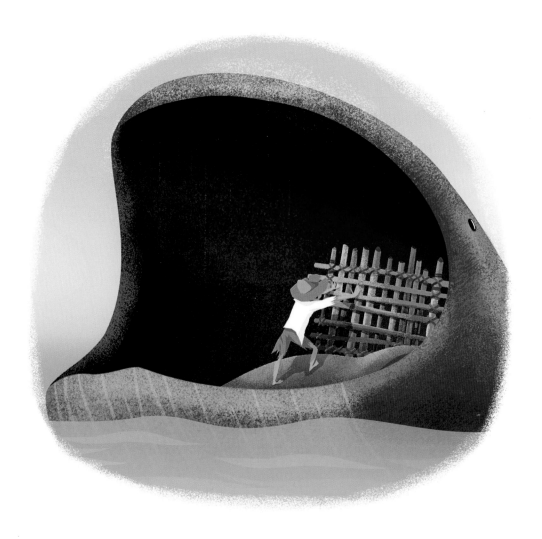

When Whale's great big mouth opened
to let him out, the man wedged the criss-cross
shape into Whale's throat...

....and leaped to shore.

"So long, Whale!" he cried out.

"I think you'll have to settle
for smaller food in the future..."

From then on, Whale couldn't
eat ANYTHING big.

He could only eat teeny tiny things, that would
fit down his throat. And that, dearest reader,
is why Whale couldn't be greedy any more.

How the
Camel got
his Hump

Long ago, in the days when the world had just begun, Camel didn't have a hump on his back as he does today.

Instead he looked like this...

This is the story, dearest reader,
of how he came to have a hump.

When the world was so new-and-all,
there was lots of work to do.
People were always busy
fetching and carrying...

...and hammering and building.
Horse, Dog and Ox helped.

They walked back and forth
in the scorching sun, working
as hard as they could.

But Camel was as **lazy** as the day was long.
He didn't work. He just stood around,
chomping on leaves in the sunshine.

Not only that, but he was **grumpy** too.

"Please can you help
me fetch sticks?"
Dog asked Camel.

HUMPH!

Camel snorted rudely,
and went right on eating.

"Please can you help
me bring branches?"
asked Horse.

Camel snorted again. Then he
stood there with his nose in the air
until Horse gave up and trudged away.

"Please can you help me pull
this heavy cart?" asked Ox.

It would be easier
with two of us.

HUMPH!

Camel shook his head.

The animals went to complain to Man.
"It's not **FAIR**," they moaned. "Camel won't help."

Man shrugged. "If Camel won't help,
you three will just have to work harder."

The animals looked at Camel
lazing around doing nothing.

And they felt really, **really** cross.

Just then, a desert storm blew up...
Out of the whirling, swirling sand,
came a magic genie.

The animals rushed up to him, hoping he could help.
"Camel does nothing, while we do all the work,"
they complained. "We wish he'd change!"

"Your wish is my command,"
said the genie.

So the genie went to find Camel.
"What's all this I hear about you
not working?" he asked.

"HUMPH!"
Camel said.

"The others have to work harder
because you're so lazy," the genie added.
"HUMPH!" said Camel again.

"Don't say that too often, or you might regret it," the genie warned. "This is your last chance, Camel. **Will you do some work?**"

"HUMPH!"

said Camel, and kept on munching.

The genie waved his arms.
There was a *zap*... *whoosh*...
flash!...

...and a big, hairy hump sprouted on Camel's back!

"WHAT'S THAT?" he gasped.

"Your HUMPH!" the genie chuckled. "It will help you work."

"How can that thing help me?" asked Camel.

The genie laughed.

"Your **humph** stores food so you won't have to eat so often."

"You can catch up on your work
while everyone else stops for lunch!"

Ever since that day, Camel has worked hard.
He still has his 'humph' on his back.

(Although these days
people call it a
'hump', so as not to
hurt his feelings.)

But he is as **grumpy** and
bad-mannered as ever.

Why the
Kangaroo
Jumps

A long, long time ago,
in a dry, dusty desert...

the first kangaroo sat on a rock
and she grumbled and grunted
and mumbled and moaned.

Kangaroo didn't like the way she looked,
with her short, stumpy legs and
her even shorter, stumpier tail.

One day, Kangaroo shouted to the gods.

WILL YOU PLEASE MAKE
ME LOOK DIFFERENT?

The gods refused, so Kangaroo kept yelling...

The gods flew to a wild dog, who was snoozing in the shade, and yelled at him.

WAKE UP!

Make Kangaroo different!

The dog sat up and smiled a wicked smile.

His beady
eyes glinted.

His sharp teeth
gleamed in the
desert sun.

And then...

Snarling and slavering, the wild dog chased
Kangaroo over sun-baked rocks and
across sun-scorched desert.

Grrrrhh...

Wailing and whimpering,
Kangaroo ran
and ran
and ran
and ran.

Aaagh!

She ran between towering mountains.

She ran through long wavy grass
and short scratchy grass.

Kangaroo ran all the way
across the desert until she reached...

Kangaroo stared at the opposite bank.
"I can't swim," she gasped.
"How will I get across?"

There was only one thing to do...

Kangaroo crouched down low on her
short stumpy legs...

The wild dog kept chasing,
and growling
and slavering
and snarling...

...and Kangaroo kept jumping.

As she jumped, her back legs
grew big and strong,
and her tail
grew fat and long.

She jumped between trees and back and forth over the river, all the way around the desert to where she began.

Then she yelled to the gods,
high in the sky.

WHY DID YOU MAKE THAT
WICKED DOG CHASE ME?

WHY?

"You wanted to be different,"
one of the gods replied.
"Now you are!"

Kangaroo had been tricked,
but the more she thought about it,
the less she minded.

In fact, she realized she was happy.

After all...
jumping was rather fun.

Designed by Laura Nelson Norris
Edited by Lesley Sims
Digital imaging: Nick Wakeford

First published in 2018 by Usborne Publishing Ltd., 83-85 Saffron Hill, London EC1N 8RT, England.
www.usborne.com. Copyright © 2018 Usborne Publishing Limited.
The name Usborne and the devices ♀🎈 are Trade Marks of Usborne Publishing Ltd.
UE First published in America in 2018.